This book belongs to:
D0513930

Contents

Peppa Pig's Family Computer

Mummy Pig is working on the family computer. She is typing very fast. Mummy Pig has a lot of important work to do today.

Daddy Pig is in the kitchen
making soup for lunch.

"Daddy?" Peppa asks. "Can we go and watch
Mummy on the computer please?"
"Yes, as long as you don't disturb her," Daddy Pig says.

"Mummy?" Peppa asks. "Can George and I sit on your lap and watch you work?"

"Yes, as long as you both sit quietly,"
Mummy Pig agrees.

About a minute later, Peppa asks, "Can we play the Happy Mrs Chicken game on the computer?"

Mummy Pig says, "We can play Happy Mrs Chicken later. But now I have to work."

Another minute later, Peppa asks, "Mummy? Can we help you work?" Peppa taps away at the computer like Mummy Pig.

“No, Peppa!” Mummy says. “You mustn’t touch the computer while I’m working.”

"Yes, George," Peppa says in a bossy voice. "You mustn't do this." Peppa taps away again and the computer flashes.

"Peppa! Stop!" Mummy Pig says.

"Sorry, Mummy," Peppa says. "I was just showing George what not to do."

"Daddy Pig!" Mummy calls. "Can you mend the computer while I finish the lunch?"

"Uh . . ." Daddy Pig says. "I'm not very good with these things."

"Hmmm . . ." Daddy Pig pushes a button.

"Mmmm . . ." Daddy Pig pushes another button.

"Maybe if I switch it off and switch it on again . . ."

Whirrr
Bzzzt
Uh-uh
Whirrr
Bzzzt

Daddy Pig has mended the computer!
"Hooray, Daddy!" shouts Peppa.

She and George jump up and down.
"Yes," Daddy Pig smiles. "I am a bit of
an expert at these things."

"Daddy," Peppa asks. "Can we play that computer game, Happy Mrs Chicken? Mummy said we could play it later," Peppa says. "And now it's later!"

"Well," Daddy Pig thinks for a moment, "okay then."
Daddy Pig starts the Happy Mrs Chicken game.

"Ho, ho, ho!" Daddy Pig laughs as Peppa and George play Happy Mrs Chicken.

"Snort!" Mummy Pig says as she comes into the room. "I see the computer is working again!"

The End

Fun at the Fair

Today, Peppa and her family are at the funfair.

"Snort! Slidey, slidey!" giggles George.

"George wants to go on the helter-skelter," says Daddy Pig.

Daddy Pig and George head off to the helter-skelter.

"Roll up! Roll up!" cries Miss Rabbit.
"Hook a duck and win a giant teddy!"
"I'll try to win one for you Peppa," says Mummy Pig. "But I don't think it's that easy!"
"It's impossible!" laughs Miss Rabbit.
"We'll see about that!" cries Mummy Pig.

Sploosh! Mummy Pig has hooked a duck!

"Hooray!" cheers Peppa.

"That's amazing!" cries Miss Rabbit.

"Here's your giant teddy!"

"Wouldn't you like a little teddy instead, Peppa?"

"No way!" giggles Peppa, happily.

George and Daddy Pig are at the helter-skelter.
"Hmm, it's a bit high, George. Are you sure you want to have a go?" asks Daddy Pig.
George giggles and runs up the stairs to the top.
It's a bit too high and George starts to cry.
"Don't worry, George. I'll come up with you," says Daddy Pig.

"Hee, hee! Weeeeeeee!" cries George,
sliding all the way down the helter-skelter.
Now, George is having too much fun to be scared.
"It is a bit high," says Daddy Pig nervously.
Daddy Pig is more scared than George.
Oops! Daddy Pig slips down the slide!

Wooahhh!

Peppa and Mummy Pig are at the
'Hit the Target' stall.

"You can do that easily, Mummy," says Peppa.

"Ho, ho! You won't win!" laughs Mr Labrador.

"Women are useless at this!"

"What did you say?" says Mummy Pig crossly.

She picks up the bow and arrow and aims . . .

Whoosh!
The arrow hits the target right in the middle.

Mummy Pig wins again!

"Unbelievable," cries Mr Labrador. "Here's your teddy!"

"Hooray!" cheers Peppa.

Now she has two giant teddies.

Daddy Pig and George are riding on the big wheel. George loves it, but Daddy Pig is a little bit scared. "This really is high!" says Daddy Pig, as the big wheel goes round and round. "Hee, hee. Snort!" giggles George.

Daddy Pig and George find Peppa and Mummy Pig.
"Hit this button with a hammer," says
Mr Bull. "If the bell rings, you win a prize!"
"I'll have a go," says Daddy Pig. "Stand back!"
"I think you're a bit wobbly from the big wheel!"
says Mummy Pig.

"Ho, ho!" laughs Mr Bull.
"Daddy Pig is looking a bit shaky!"

"What?" says Mummy Pig, crossly.

"Give . . . me . . . that . . . hammer!"

Whack! Mummy Pig hits the button

as hard as she can.

The bell rings loudly. Ding! Ding! Ding!

Everyone is very impressed. Mummy Pig wins all the giant teddies at the fair! "Hooray!" cheers Peppa and she gives all of her friends one giant teddy bear each. "Hooray!" everyone cheers. "We love funfairs!"

The End

George's First Day at Playgroup

Today is George's first day at playgroup.
"Isn't George too small for playgroup?" asks Peppa.
"You can look after him," says Daddy Pig.
Peppa isn't sure she wants George at
her playgroup, but she likes the idea of
looking after him.

"Are you sure George is big enough?"
Peppa asks when they arrive.
"Yes, he'll be fine," replies Daddy Pig.
"OK. He can come," says Peppa.
She holds onto George's hand.
"Grunt! Grunt!" snorts George, jumping
up and down.

Here is Madame Gazelle, Peppa's playgroup teacher. She looks after Peppa and her friends.
Madame Gazelle tells the children that George is coming to play.
The children are all very excited about meeting Peppa's little brother.

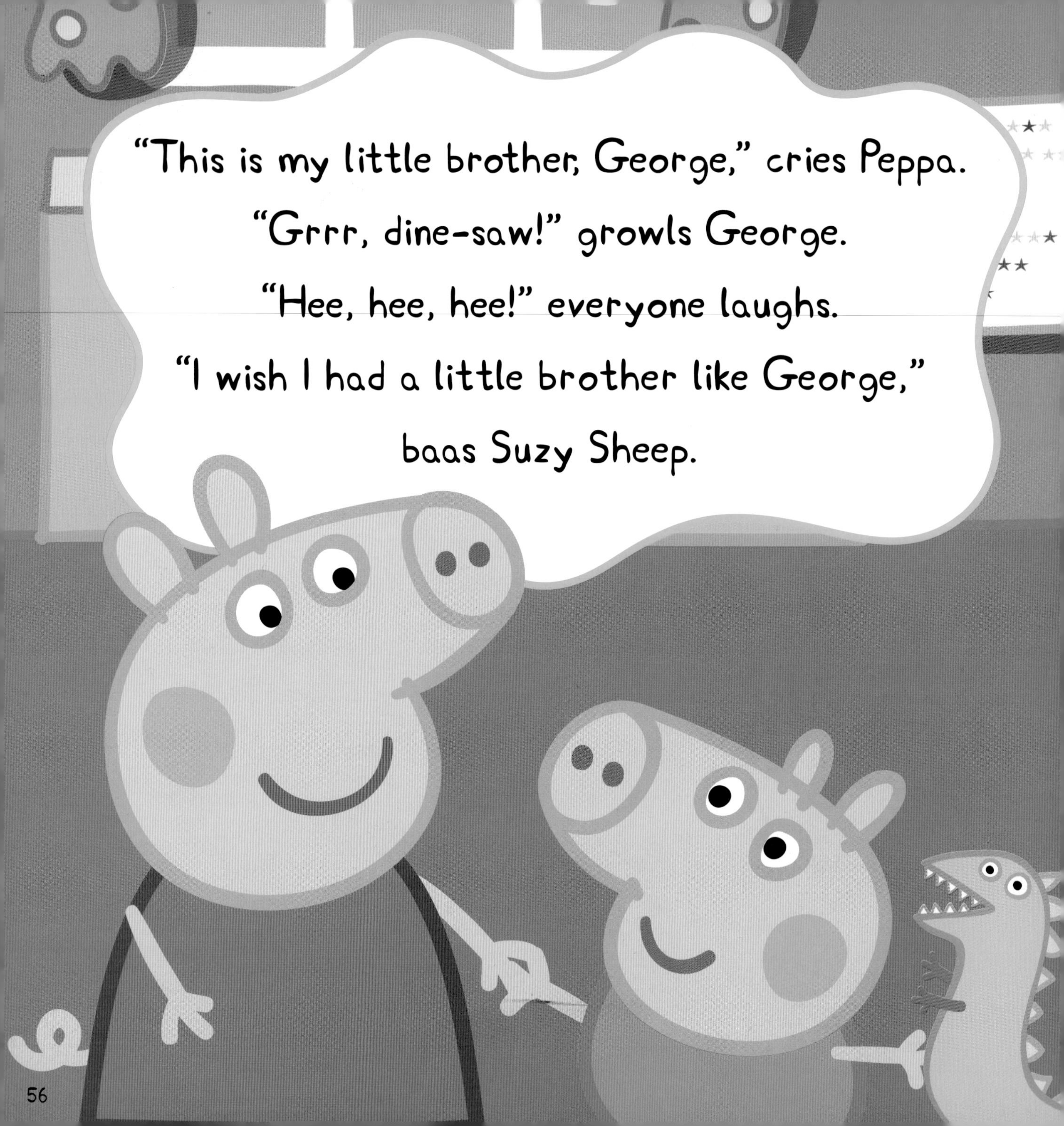
"This is my little brother, George," cries Peppa.
"Grrr, dine-saw!" growls George.
"Hee, hee, hee!" everyone laughs.
"I wish I had a little brother like George,"
baas Suzy Sheep.

1.25
1
0.75
0.5
0.25
123
A
B
C
E

E

George shakes his toy, Mr Dinosaur, at Madame Gazelle, "Grrr! Dine-saw!"

"Aah! Really scary!" laughs Madame Gazelle.

Peppa is proud of George making everyone laugh. "George is my little brother. He's brilliant," she says.

"Shall we show George how we paint pictures?" Madame Gazelle asks the children.

"George is not very good at
painting," says Peppa.
"But I can show him
how to paint a flower."
1.25
1
0.75
0.5
1
2
3

"Watch me, George," snorts Peppa.
"First, you paint a big circle."
Peppa carefully dips her brush into a pot of pink paint and draws a big pink circle right in the middle of her paper.

5
25
C

George draws a big green circle.

"No George. That's the wrong colour," snorts Peppa. "Watch me."

Peppa makes yellow petal shapes.

George paints a green zigzag.

"George! That's the wrong shape," says Peppa.

Peppa admires her flower painting.
"Perfect," she says, happily.
George is still painting. Instead of a stalk and leaves he has painted another circle with five lines sticking out from it.
"You are doing it all wrong!" says Peppa.

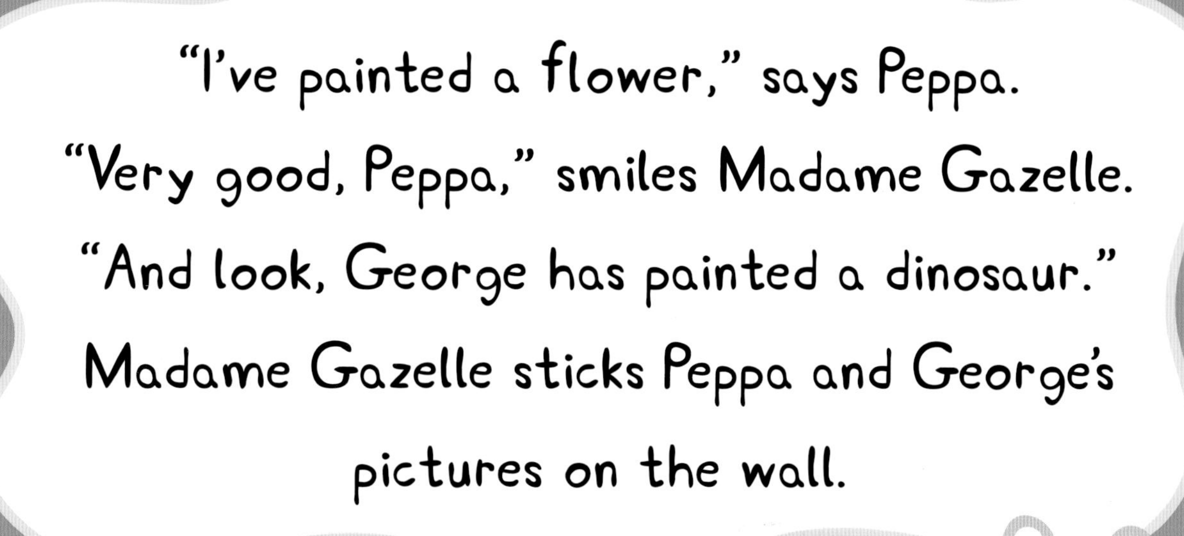

"I've painted a flower," says Peppa.

"Very good, Peppa," smiles Madame Gazelle.

"And look, George has painted a dinosaur."

Madame Gazelle sticks Peppa and George's pictures on the wall.

Now, it is time to go home.
"What will you paint next time, George?" asks Madame Gazelle.
"Dine-saw! Grrr!" giggles George.
"Hee, hee, hee!" everyone laughs.

1.25
1
0.75
0.5
0.25

The End

Peppa Plays Football

It's a sunny day and Peppa Pig and Suzy Sheep are playing tennis. "To you, Suzy!" cheers Peppa, hitting the ball. Now, it's Suzy's turn. "To you, Peppa!" she cries, hitting the ball straight over Peppa's head. Oh dear!

"Waaaa!" George feels a bit left out.

"Sorry, George," says Peppa. "You can't play tennis. We only have two racquets."

"George can be the ball boy!" cheers Suzy.

"Being a ball boy is a very important job, George," says Peppa.

Peppa and Suzy are having lots of fun,
but they keep missing the ball.
"Ball boy!" they shout together.
"Huff, puff!" George is not having fun.
He keeps running to get the ball and
he is very tired!

"Hello, everyone," cries Peppa when her friends arrive. "We're playing tennis."

"Can we play too?" asks Danny Dog.

"There aren't enough racquets," replies Suzy Sheep.

"Let's play football then,"
says Danny Dog.
"Football! Hooray!"
everyone cheers.

"We can play girls against boys," says Peppa.

"Each team needs a goalkeeper," says Danny Dog.

"Me, me!" shouts Pedro Pony.

"Me, me!" cries Rebecca Rabbit.

Pedro Pony and Rebecca Rabbit
decide to be the goalkeepers.
"The boys' team will start!" says Danny Dog.
Richard Rabbit gets the ball and runs
very fast, right by Peppa Pig,
Suzy Sheep and Candy Cat
and straight up to the . . .

. . . "GOAL!" cry Danny and Pedro together, as Richard Rabbit kicks the ball straight past Rebecca Rabbit and into the net.

"The boy is a winner!" cheers Danny Dog.

"That's not fair, we weren't ready," moans Peppa.

Rebecca Rabbit picks up the ball and runs.

"Hey!" shouts Danny Dog.

"That's cheating! You can't hold the ball."

"Yes I can!" says Rebecca. "I'm the goalkeeper."

Rebecca throws the ball into the goal,

straight past Pedro Pony.

"GOAL!" she cries.

"That goal is not allowed," says Pedro.

"Yes, it is," says Peppa.

"No, it isn't!" barks Danny.

"What a lot of noise," snorts Daddy Pig.

"I'll be the referee.
The next team to
get a goal will win
the game."

Richard Rabbit and George run off with the football, while everyone is still talking.

"Where's the ball?" asks Peppa.

But it's too late! Richard Rabbit kicks the ball straight into the goal, past Pedro Pony.

"Hooray! The boys win!" cries Danny.

"Football is a silly game," sighs Peppa, disappointed.
"Just a moment," says Daddy Pig. "The boys scored in their own goal, that means the girls win!"

"Really?" gasp all the girls. "Hooray!"

"Football is a great game!" cheers Peppa.

"Ha, ha, ha!" everyone laughs.

The End

Peppa's First Sleepover

Peppa is going to her very first sleepover at Zoe Zebra's house. "Welcome to my sleepover!" Zoe says.

"I'll pick you up in the morning," Mummy Pig says to Peppa with a kiss.

Rebecca Rabbit, Suzy Sheep and
Emily Elephant are already here.
"I've got my teddy," Peppa says.

Zoe has her monkey. Rebecca has her carrot.
Suzy has her owl. And Emily has her frog.

"Don't stay up too late, girls! And don't be too loud. Daddy Zebra has to get up early to deliver the post," Mummy Zebra says as she turns out the lights.

Zoe's baby twin sisters, Zuzu and Zaza,
want to join the sleepover too.
"Sleepovers are only for big girls!" Zoe says.

The twins begin to cry.
"They're so sweet and little," Peppa says.

"Can they stay?" Rebecca asks.
"Okay," Zoe says to the twins.
"But you must NOT fall asleep."

"What should we do first?"
Suzy asks.
"I'm having piano lessons!
Listen . . ." Zoe starts to pound
on the keys. "Twinkle, twinkle,
little star . . . "

Mummy Zebra has woken up.
"Shush! You must be quiet so Daddy Zebra can sleep!
Now, into your sleeping bags, please."

"Snort! What do we do now?" Peppa asks.
"At sleepovers, there's always
a midnight feast!" Zoe says.
"It's when we eat things," Suzy says
in a hushed voice. "In secret."

"Shh!" Zoe says as she leads the girls to the kitchen. They each grab some delicious fruit, perfect for a midnight feast. The floorboard creaks.

Oh no! Mummy Zebra has woken up. "You'll wake Daddy Zebra! Now, who knows a bedtime story?"

The girls take turns: "Once upon a time, there was a little fairy . . ." Suzy begins.

"And she lived in the forest . . ." Peppa continues.
"And the fairy met a big monster, who went . . .
RAARRR!" Emily says with a big
elephant trumpet noise!

Oh dear. The noise has woken Daddy Zebra!
"Sorry Daddy," Zoe says. "There was a story about a fairy and a scary monster."

"And we want to know what happens next!" Peppa says. "Very well," Daddy Zebra sighs. "The monster lifted up his great, big hairy paws . . ."

"And walked along on his great, big hairy feet . . . And sang . . . 'Twinkle, twinkle, little star, how I wonder what you are . . .'"
Daddy Zebra sings gently as he plays the piano.

Daddy Zebra's song has sent everyone to sleep.

The End

Sports Day

Today is school sports day.

Peppa and her
friends are all here.

The first event is running.

The children have to run as fast as they can.

“Ready . . . Steady . . . Go!”
says Madame Gazelle.

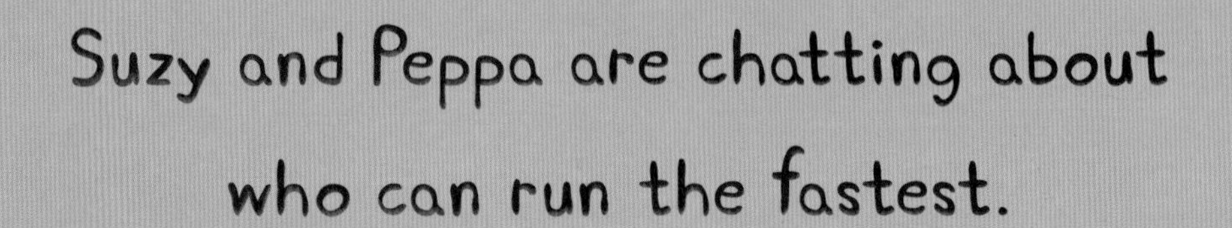

Suzy and Peppa are chatting about who can run the fastest.

Rebecca Rabbit is in the lead.

Peppa and Suzy are right at the back.

Rebecca Rabbit wins the race!

"Hooray!" everyone cheers.

Peppa and Suzy are last.

"It's not the winning that matters,"
Daddy Pig reminds them.
"But the taking part."

"The next event is the long jump," says Madame Gazelle.

George and Richard Rabbit have to run
and then jump as far as they can.
Whoever jumps the furthest is the winner.

"Ready . . . Steady . . . Go!"

Oh dear. Richard Rabbit has jumped further than George. "Hooray!" shout all his friends.

George is not happy.

"Remember, George," says Peppa. "It's not the winning that matters but the taking part."

The next race is the relay. Daddy Pig is in the lead. He hands the baton to Peppa.

"Thank you, Daddy, you did very well.
Now it's my turn to . . . " begins Peppa.
"Stop talking and run!" snorts Daddy Pig.

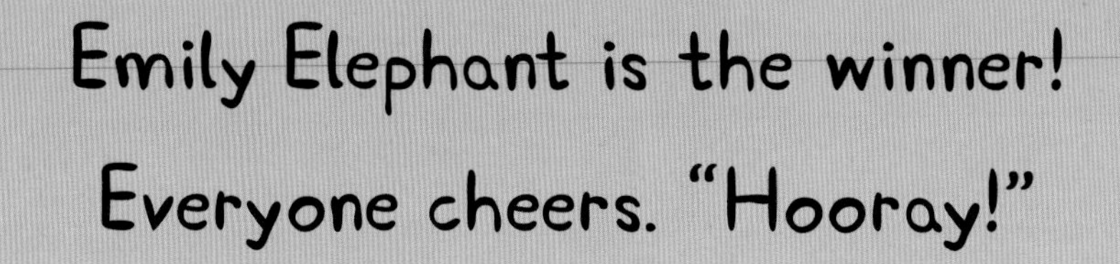

Emily Elephant is the winner!
Everyone cheers. "Hooray!"

Peppa comes last.

She is not feeling happy.

It's the last event of the day, the tug of war.

Boys against girls.

"The girls will win!" snorts Peppa.

"Woof! No they won't!" says Danny.

Everyone is pulling so hard, the rope breaks!

"The result is a draw!
Both teams win!" says Madame Gazelle.
Everybody cheers.

"Hooray!"

"I love school sports day," snorts Peppa,

"Especially when I win a prize!"

The End